MARIE-HÉLÈNE LEBEAULT

AUTHOR OF THE EVERS SERIES

A SUMMER

— OF —

UNITY

DEFENDERS OF THE REALM - NOVELLA FIVE

BEACHES AND TRAILS
PUBLISHING

About the Author

Marie-Helene Lebeault lives in Quebec, Canada and is the mother of two young adults. A retired teacher, she now spends her days writing, translating academic manuals, and lending her voice to corporate training videos. She enjoys reading, hiking, and going to the beach. She is also an avid rollercoaster fiend and is on a mission to visit all the Six Flags amusement parks with her daughter. Every year, she travels for three weeks on a solo adventure to a new part of the world.

Follow on Social Media, she'd love to hear from you!

Website Email Newsletter

facebook.com/mhlebeaultauthor

x.com/mhlebeault

instagram.com/mhlebeault

amazon.com/author/mhlebeault

bookbub.com/authors/marie-helene-lebeault

goodreads.com/mhlebeault

linkedin.com/in/mhlebeault

tiktok.com/@mhlebeaultauthor

youtube.com/@mhlebeault

Also by the Author

Blood Magick

Blood Legacy

Standalones

Clarity Castle

What Happens Next?

Ghost Stories

Holiday Shifters

Echoes of Tomorrow

Utopia

Picture Books

Fairy Grandmother: Millie Goes to Antarctica

Fairy Grandmother: Millie Goes to the North Pole

Fairy Grandmother: Millie Goes to China

Fairy Grandmother: Millie Goes to Africa

(Also available in French, Spanish, German, and Italian)

CHAPTER
ONE

Queen Rowena stretched her arms over her head, sighing as the carriage settled to a stop. It was the third day of her journey from the Eldavon palace back to her own home in Odentia. The events of the past few months were finally over, and she was looking forward to the tedium of the journey before she had to resume her royal duties.

"We could keep going through the night," her husband, Hector, said as he gazed out of the window.

Her husband. It still seemed so strange to say that, even though they had been married for some time now. In Odentia, marriages were private, intimate affairs; it was the announcements that were grand. A couple sometimes could be married for years before they announced it. They had just had their second wedding, a celebration in Eldavon according to their traditions.

But they had not yet lived as husband and wife.

Rowena cleared her throat, shaking off those thoughts. "I would prefer to stop for the night. I can't read when the carriage jostles all over the place."

Hector nodded.

The footman opened the carriage door and Hector descended first. Traditionally, this was so that the queen would have more time to put herself in order after being in the privacy of the carriage. Truthfully, though, it was to give the soldiers more time to ensure there were no hidden assassins in the area.

Rowena came out of the carriage and was hurried straight to her and Hector's tent. She sighed once she was inside. It would be lovely to walk through the forest a little and stretch her legs. The last time she made this journey, though, she was kidnapped and so she couldn't blame anyone for their extra precautions.

Her tent was very roomy, anyway. There was a bed that was set up every night and taken down again in the morning, covered in thick quilts and pillows. Her maids already waited next to a privacy screen, which she stepped behind. Her traveling gown was simple and comfortable, but she still breathed a sigh of relief when they released her stays. After changing into a fresh chemise, she pulled a modest nightgown over her head and dismissed them.

Hector, coming out from behind his privacy screen, was likewise dressed for sleep now. His fluffy brown hair, neither straight nor curly, stood up on end. He smiled at her, the corners of his silver eyes turning up even more than usual. He always looked like he was smiling, so every time he actually smiled, it made his whole face brighten.

"So, you want to read tonight?" he asked as he took a seat on the little desk that held his writing supplies.

"It's better to stay up as long as I can, so I can sleep during the day," Rowena offered.

Hector nodded, then cleared his throat. "I was wondering if maybe we could talk a little."

Rowena gratefully pulled a chair over closer to him. "Yes, that would be fantastic."

Hector nodded, his tanned cheeks turning dark with a blush. "So. What do you want to talk about?"

Rowena laughed, her own cheeks turning warm. "You sound so awkward! We agreed to this arrangement because we felt so at ease with each other. I know that marriage changes things, but I hope not that much."

"You always did like to tease me." Hector chuckled as he shook his head. "Very well. Then how are you feeling, now that you've gone through the Silver Springs?"

"Wonderful," Rowena answered honestly.

She leaned back in her chair and stretched out her neck from side to side, her long, loose curls falling from side to side. She'd worn them in tight braids the whole day and was glad to have the release on her scalp.

"It's so different from when I could access a dragon," she said. The villainous Silas had briefly stolen the dragon from another person and given it to her. "It always felt as easy as breathing to be a dragon, but also uncomfortable, somehow. Like wearing someone else's clothes, even if they fit you."

Hector nodded, his silver eyes locked on her face.

"It feels the same as ever, yet so different," Rowena said slowly.

The Silver Springs, once drank from, allowed a person to access their innate magic. It revealed a person as a witch with silver hair, a dragon with silver eyes, or a human with no visual change.

"I feel powerful." Rowena looked at her hands. "I can't really describe it. But I feel the steadiness of the earth beneath me and I know that I am just as steady. I've never been so certain of myself."

Hector smiled again. "That's how I felt when I went through the Springs. I never thought I would be a dragon, but when I saw my silver eyes, I knew it was right. I'm glad that you feel peace with yours."

He grasped her hand in his and squeezed lightly. Rowena shifted a little closer, enjoying the feeling of his hand in hers. As the only child of the old king, she had been raised to be queen. She couldn't remember a time in her life when she didn't have the weight of her responsibilities on her shoulders. With Hector, though, she felt almost like a regular person.

"I'm glad that Silas has been defeated," Hector said absently as he traced his fingers over her knuckles. "Now we can finally get back to life as it should be."

"I'm glad the four rulers of Eldavon believed me when I told them all my actions were because I was playing a role, to be able to stop him," Rowena said fervently. She shivered as she remembered the last few months. It would take some time to fix the damage he left behind. "But we were able to stop him. And we will make things better."

Hector nodded. They were silent a little while longer, each lost in their own thoughts. Rowena eventually read while Hector scratched out letters to his very extended family. It was peaceful as the sounds of night fell outside their tent. Rowena grew restless, though, and did some simple stretches and weight training since she knew the guards would not like it if she left the tent.

"Do you want to dance?" Hector asked her.

Rowena glanced around the tent. "I'm not sure we have enough room for that."

Hector stood and began moving things to the sides of the tent. "We have plenty of room."

"We have no music."

Hector started to hum and held his hand out to her. His eyes twinkled and Rowena couldn't resist. She took his hand and they started to spin throughout the tent, singing and dancing until they were both breathless. As they slowed, Hector's arms stole slowly around her.

"Rowena..." He bent his head toward her. "This is our honeymoon."

Her heart started to hammer, but Rowena nodded. Once they returned to Odentia, she would be too busy to take the customary month. So, this trip was the best they had.

"May I kiss you?" her husband whispered.

Rowena lifted her face toward his. "You may."

Hector smiled as he kissed her for the first time.

THE TRIP REMAINED UNEVENTFUL. Every day was much the same, only Rowena and Hector asked for fewer things to be unpacked every night so they had more room in the tent. Instead, they ended up dancing away the night, aided by a music box that Hector bought at a small village they passed.

Despite nothing happening—or perhaps because of it—Rowena found this calm time with her new husband exhilarating. She had already known him quite well before the match was arranged, but now that she was able to speak more freely with him, she found that his kindness went even deeper than she realized.

Once in Odentia, Rowena ordered a day's detour toward a lake and hot springs. Though they couldn't afford too much of a delay, she wanted to stay two nights near the water, where they could have a break from the jostling carriage. She wanted to move and stretch her muscles.

The hot springs were within a small grotto, open to the west. Rowena, dressed in her bathing suit, lounged in the sunset as the heat from the pools dripped off her arms. She and Hector had swum all day in the lake and her muscles ached pleasantly from the exertion.

"The way Odentia royalty works means you are expected to have children, doesn't it?" Hector asked. He pulled himself from the pool to sit next to her. The light cloth of his bathing suit clung to his chest.

"Yes. But even if it weren't expected, I would want children," Rowena answered.

Hector frowned at the sunset. "It seems so wrong to me, to say a person must use their life in a certain way."

"Is it so different from dragons being expected to be protectors in Eldavon?" Rowena challenged.

"Maybe not."

Rowena pulled her knees to her chest and wrapped her arms around them, watching him. It occurred to her that she didn't know... "Do you want children?"

"Oh, yes. I want as many as possible. But," he added with a chuckle, "it's a decision we'll have to make together."

"Three. That's how many I want." Her cheeks burned as she cleared her throat. "And I want our first to be soon."

Hector's eyes widened. Rowena gave him an encouraging smile as she reached for his hands.

"Can I kiss you?" she asked.

Hector swallowed and nodded.

Rowena rolled to her knees. And she shared her second kiss with her husband.

CHAPTER
TWO

Hector peered through the curtains of the carriage, careful not to let in too much light. Rowena lay stretched out on the opposite bench, sleeping peacefully. Her long, midnight-black hair was in traveling braids, pinned in place beneath a crocheted bonnet. They were almost to the capitol, where they both would be expected to ride in on horses rather than in the carriage.

It was a strange feeling, being married to someone who wasn't his fated mate. Even stranger that Rowena expected to have an arranged marriage from the time she was young. He didn't understand this whole obsession with a generational ruler. Just because a parent was a good ruler didn't mean their child would be.

Or, in Rowena's case, just because her father was a selfish king didn't mean she would be a selfish queen.

His thoughts were broken through by shouting, followed by the clash of metal against metal. Rowena jerked awake.

"What's happening?" she cried.

The door to the carriage ripped open. Hector kicked the face of the strange man that appeared there. He stumbled back but dropped a smoldering torch into the carriage. The light cotton flooring quickly caught fire. Hector's lips pulled back into a snarl as he wrapped his arms around Rowena and pulled her through the rising flames.

Rowena clung to him as they stumbled free of the burning carriage. Hector's eyes streamed from the smoke. Bile rose up his throat as he got a look around; they were under attack, the guards circling the carriages while servants raced for cover.

"Get the queen and kill the dragon," someone shouted.

Several people raced at them, naked swords in hand. Hector roared as he lifted Rowena back behind him. They would not put their hands on her!

He summoned his dragon. Red scales burst over his skin as the first sword came at him; it clattered against his armor and skittered aside. Wings snapped open behind him and he let out a roar, spitting fire into the air. The shouts turned to screams and even the guards raced away from him.

A group of the attackers gathered together. One of them aimed an arrow at him; with a single flick of his tail, he bowled them over. Then he pounced, snatching them all up in his clawed feet. He rolled them together, knocking free their weapons, and pressed his forearm along them, pinning them in place. They all stared up at him with wide eyes as they struggled against his hold.

It was only then that he realized he didn't have the means to tell anyone to come bind them. He growled, his head swinging toward the guards but they only flinched and backed away from him. His head swung the other way, facing Rowena.

He scanned the area, making sure none of the attackers were near enough to hurt her. Even if they seemed to be unconscious, they might just be biding their time. Then he finally looked at her. She appeared unharmed and relief flooded through him.

Her lady's maids had joined her and she stared at him, eyes wide. Her face was ashen as her hands curled into her skirt. She trembled where she stood, as though she was fighting the urge to run.

A cold feeling ran through Hector's body. Was she afraid of him?

Rowena shook herself. "Bind the rebels. We will take them back to the palace."

Despite her order, it still took the guards a few minutes before they moved forward. Hector released the rebels one at a time, allowing the guards to bind them. His stomach churned whenever one of them flinched back from him. These were all people he had spent a good deal of time with. Did they think he would turn on them, just because he inhabited a different body now?

Perhaps there was more work to be done than he realized.

THEY ENTERED the capitol city with as much fanfare as Hector expected. The burned royal carriage was being pulled into the city in another way, along with the prisoners. Hector watched the crowd with sharp eyes, searching for any sign that Rowena might be attacked again. The people seemed to be very pleased to see their queen. They cheered her name and waved at her.

Hector couldn't help but notice the looks thrown at him were tentative at best, and distrustful at worst. He tried to soften his expression, but he remained so tense that he knew that they would think he was a hard, humorless man.

Once they were back at the palace, he wanted to go to the prisons so he could interrogate the rebels. They had known where the procession would be and when—which meant that Rowena could be in more danger yet.

"Rowena," he said as he jogged up to her.

His breath left his lungs when her shoulders sagged. The smile that had been on her face all the ride here disappeared and her hands shook. He took them in his own, wincing. She'd been more shaken than he realized.

"Yes?" she asked, gazing up at him.

Hector hesitated, then shook his head. She had guards for a reason —no doubt the rebels would be questioned by others. "Let's get you to your room to rest."

Rowena opened her mouth, then closed it again.

"That is... if you're still okay being alone with me," Hector said slowly.

Rowena blinked twice. A furrow formed on her brow. "Why wouldn't I be okay with being alone with you?"

Hector ducked his head, unwilling to admit his fears.

They went to her chambers—a lavish, ornate sitting room with a bedroom and bathing room attached—and Rowena pulled him to sit on a couch next to her. Her dark eyes were unfocused as she stared at a huge window that led to the balcony.

"I never thought they would be so angry as to attack. To try to kill you." Rowena shuddered as she turned her gaze to him. "I'm so sorry for pulling you into this."

Hector searched her eyes. "You're not afraid of my dragon?"

Her brows pinched. "No. Of course not. But if you had remained in Eldavon, people wouldn't try to kill you."

All of his breath left at once. Hector pressed his forehead to Rowena's, relief singing through him. "I thought..."

"We'll have to reassure them somehow. Stop this irrational hatred. I just don't know how. If my uncle was here, he'd know what to do," she murmured.

Finnegan was stuck in Eldavon, living at the Silver Springs; in the course of defeating Silas, he had ended up with a Gorgon curse on him, turning him into a statue unless he was bathed in those sacred waters.

"I guess this is part of being a queen," Rowena sighed. "I'll have to figure it out on my own."

Hector brought her palm to his lips. "You aren't alone, Rowena. I'm here. And I will always protect you," he promised.

Rowena stroked his cheek, shivering. "But who will protect you?"

He shot her a cocky grin, relaxing his muscles. "I'm a dragon. I can protect myself."

Rowena didn't look appeased. "There is always some danger with being in the public eye. Whether it's politics or commerce. Ever since I was young, I was taught the dangers of the people. I was foolish to think that this change wouldn't cause an upset."

"On the bright side, they seemed more interested in kidnapping than assassinating you," Hector joked weakly.

It seemed to be enough to shake Rowena out of whatever thoughts she'd gotten lost in. She sent him a dirty look and leaned forward to pull her shoes off. "We'll have to change that. We're going to need to do something to show them that we have their best interests in mind. I know how my father would react to this—and they have to see that I care. And that caring doesn't make me weak."

"Why would they think that caring was a weakness?" Hector asked, his eyes widening in shock.

Rowena tossed her shoes away. "My father did. But I don't want to talk about him anymore. So. Eldavon is expecting us to start sending people over to drink from the Silver Springs. How are we going to select them?"

Hector gazed with admiration at his wife and queen. It would be all too easy to fall apart after what happened on the road today, but she was already pulling herself together for the good of her kingdom.

Things were still rocky. Even without Silas's interference, there was a long, painful history between Odentia and Eldavon. They had a lot of work to do if they were going to fix the wrongs of the past.

"We need to make sure that everyone in the kingdom has equal opportunity to go," he said. Then he grinned at her. "I have a few ideas for that."

CHAPTER
THREE

Rowena never felt fully at ease in her council chambers. Right up until his death, her father hoped that he would have a boy to carry on his legacy. It was an archaic way of thinking, that sons made the best heirs, but nobody would ever say her father was forward-thinking. Rowena hoped that with the Earth magic flowing through her from drinking the Silver Springs, she would feel more like she belonged here.

She was disappointed. As soon as she stepped into her council chambers and nodded in greeting to the waiting Lords—all men and nobody in rank below that of Earl—she felt just as unprepared as she always did.

Hector walked right behind her and she drew strength and comfort from his presence. He might not have a full understanding of how things happened here in Odentia, but he was learning quickly.

Today, he wore the blue uniform he'd been given when he trained at the Institute. Rowena wore the traditional high-waisted green gown of the queen. The bodice and skirt were heavily embroidered with gold images of the sun, a symbol usually worn by the king. She was the ruler of this land, after all, and her garb needed to reflect that.

"Your Majesty," Duke Volka said with a kindly smile and bowed toward her. "We are all pleased to see you return. Ah, and I see you brought His Royal Highness." He bowed at Hector, who stepped in behind Rowena, though the bow wasn't as deep as it was for her. "I trust you are both settling in after your journey?"

"We are, thank you," Rowena said. "Now, I'm afraid I must be terribly rude. We will forgo the usual pleasantries and get down to business. The rebels who attacked me and my husband yesterday. Have their reasons been uncovered?"

She settled into her chair, Hector taking his spot next to her. The Council Lords seemed to be slightly disgruntled with her boldness, but most hid it well. Duke Volka twined his hands together on the table, his expression growing somber.

"Indeed, we have," he said. "Ever since your marriage to Prince Hector, there have been rumors abounding that Eldavon means to overturn your throne. Since the actions of the wizard Silas, these rumors have expanded."

"How so?" Hector asked.

Duke Volka frowned at him. "Many now believe that you intend to steal the Queen's crown and proclaim yourself king. Or, at the very least, manipulate her into doing your bidding."

Rowena suppressed a groan. It was a risk from the start, she knew that, but the whole idea was so ludicrous! If Eldavon truly wanted to annex Odentia, they would simply do it. Despite the difficulties they'd suffered the last few years, they were still a people full of magic. It would be easy for their armies to crush any of the surrounding kingdoms if they had a mind to do it.

Luckily for everyone, that wasn't the Eldavon way. They weren't a violent culture.

"But I'm not," Hector protested. "I don't want to be king."

"Nonetheless, it is what more and more people believe," Volka answered silkily.

"And that's why they attacked," Rowena murmured. "They were acting from a misguided attempt to protect me."

As nice as it was to hear that the people supported her, the cost was beyond the pale. This wasn't the sort of start she wanted with her reign. Volka started to say something but Rowena held up her hand, thinking hard.

"We will have to have an official ball for Hector to be introduced as the Prince Consort," she said slowly. They had planned for one after their initial wedding, but Silas cut that short.

Volka shifted in his seat and a few of the other Lords scowled. But Rowena wasn't expecting Hector of all people to protest the idea.

"Is that wise at this time? There's so much work to be done," he said, a furrow in his brow.

"We need to establish your place as my husband. There's no better way to do that than a ball," Rowena answered, keeping her tone steady.

Hector ran a hand through his brown hair. "But won't having a big celebration focused on me make the people even more certain that I'm here to steal your crown?"

Lord Rutledge, a burly, sharp-eyed man, snorted. "What would you suggest then?"

"Use the funds that would be used for a ball to improve the standard of living in the kingdom," Hector answered readily. "And get everything into a regular rhythm. Start living our lives as normal once again."

Rowena took his hand in hers, shaking her head. "This is normal, Hector. It's an Odentia tradition and one that we must adhere to. If we don't present you to the people as Prince Consort, then they will think that you're trying to hide something."

"I hadn't thought of it like that," Hector said.

Rutledge passed a disapproving look over him. "In that same vein, you need to be rid of that blue uniform of yours and start wearing proper Odentia garb. You look as though you're one of their soldiers."

Hector frowned at him. "These clothes are specially created to keep with me when I shift to my dragon form and back. Odentia clothes won't survive the shift."

"And you think you have reason to shift in the palace?" Rutledge challenged.

Volka snorted. "If you put him in our garb, it'll just look like he's putting on a show. We need deeper connections than clothes if he is to be accepted by the people."

Rowena listened as the lords started to debate among themselves. Not one of them looked at her or asked her what she thought. She felt as though she was a child again rather than a queen of twenty-three years, married, and responsible for the kingdom. She felt herself slumping backward into her chair and forced herself to straighten.

There was one thing that her father always said that she still believed; a ruler had no place for self-doubt if they were going to be successful.

She stood, and the lords all hurried to scrape back their chairs to stand with her. They all fell silent as they watched her.

"Since Hector's intentions are being questioned so deeply, we will have to make an effort to counter that," she said, ignoring the current debate about clothing. "At the ball, he will take oaths to me, to serve and protect me as his queen, to assay the fears. That will be enough to deal with the current unrest, will it not?"

"For some," Rutledge rumbled.

Rowena nodded her acknowledgment. But she didn't consider it too much more; there was very little that could be done to convince everyone. Some would never be convinced, even if Hector gave his life to protect her. She wasn't going to be pulled into a drawn-out debate as to all the possibilities of what they could or would do.

She took her seat again. "Now. We have many other things to discuss. The agreement I made with Eldavon means that—"

"Forgive me, your Majesty," Earl Sand interrupted. "But this matter is far from closed. These rebels may have been acting in your defense, but the fact remains they attacked a royal procession. There will be others. You need to show a stronger force and deal with these traitors. The way your father would have done."

Rowena's stomach churned at the thought. She gripped the armrests of her chairs as she stared Sand down. "I will not attack my own people. They have been arrested, they have been imprisoned. If they can be made to understand, they will be freed. I will not be a bloody queen."

Sand's lips pressed together. "Showing weakness will only put us all in danger."

"It's not weak to show mercy," Hector said.

Rowena opened her mouth to interject but never got the chance. Sand leapt to his feet, glaring at Hector. The hostility rolling off him made Rowena flinch. What had Hector done to receive such wrath?

"Maybe your Eldavon kindness works when it's backed by the threats of dragons," he snarled. "But Odentia has no such luxury! Are you going to shield us if they come at us with guillotines, the way they killed the nobility across the sea?"

"Sit down," Volka snapped. "That revolution happened because the ruling classes spent far too much time on their shows of wealth and strength while the people starved. Your examples are folly."

Rowena clenched her hands together. She reached inside of herself, drawing on that inner strength that she'd been enveloped in after she drank from the Silver Springs. But when she opened her mouth to speak, she was interrupted yet again. Years of instinct, of being shouted at by her father every time she dared interrupt, reared their heads like a hydra.

Maybe they were right.

Maybe she wasn't cut out to be queen.

Maybe Odentia would be better off under the rule of someone else.

FOUR

Hector rubbed his tired eyes. Though the curtains were open to allow light into Rowena's study, the windows were narrow and they had to have several lanterns hanging about to give them enough light to work. It was meant to be a safety feature to have such small windows, but Hector thought it made daily work rather difficult.

"I think it's ready," Rowena said as she pored over the speech she'd been writing for several days now. "It explains the purpose of selecting citizens to go to the Silver Springs as well as fully sharing the process of how people will be selected."

"It does that," Hector agreed slowly.

He leaned back in his chair and gazed at Rowena. Her black curls were pulled into a braided bun at the nape of her neck, held in place by a glittering golden net. She wore a tunic and trousers today; they were both pale lavender and the trouser legs were wide enough to look like a skirt while allowing her more freedom of movement.

A knowing smile hovered on her lips. "But?"

"But I have an issue with the process of selection," Hector admitted reluctantly.

Rowena and the Eldavon kings and queens were working together for this; he was meant to use mind-to-mind to report back on the selection process to get Eldavon's feedback, though they were not going to override Rowena's decisions in this matter. He knew that they wouldn't approve of this method, either.

"I thought that people submitting their willingness to be part of it was a good idea," Rowena said.

"Yes, but you have to understand that the poor education of many Odentia people means that they aren't able to write into the palace," Hector said slowly. "Not to mention, there are a lot of stops along the way for people with the means to interfere. Also, most of the working people are going to find it difficult to leave jobs their families depend on to take part in this."

Rowena frowned at her speech. "So, what you're saying is that this still weighs heavily toward the nobility. And you're just bringing it up now."

Hector sighed. "To be fair, I'm only now hearing what method of selection you've been planning."

"I have to ensure that the people I send are loyal to the crown. What if I send a bunch of rebels and they become dragons?" Rowena challenged.

"The Silver Springs is meant to be an equalizing process. It's not fair to keep such rigid social hierarchies," Hector said.

Rowena pursed her lips. "You mean to say that Odentia society is unfair and—"

She cut herself off, breathing in through her nose.

Hector slowly got to his feet. "In comparison to what I'm used to… yes. It feels very unfair to me, Rowena. But I don't think that this discussion is going to get anywhere at the moment. I'm still not sleeping well and we've been stuck in here for hours. I'm going to go to the gardens and get some fresh air and exercise. Will you come with me?"

"I have work to do," Rowena said flatly.

Hector nodded, fighting back the instinct to tell her she was overworking herself. He left the study, heading out to the gardens. The sunshine helped his head feel much clearer. As he was moving through a few basic fighting moves, two courtiers came walking down the path toward him.

"Prince Hector," the man said with a bow. "I don't know if you remember me. I'm Lord Nathanial Corella. This is my wife, Lady Cassidy."

"A pleasure," Lady Cassidy cooed, batting her lashes at him.

Hector made himself smile politely. He even bowed toward them, though he wanted nothing more than to scowl and walk away. He'd come out here to try to release some of his stress, to be able to help Rowena. Or, at the very least, clear his mind enough to listen to her.

The Corellas were vocal in their opposition to him marrying Rowena at all. Now they were all simpering smiles and friendly demeanors. All fake, but he was Prince Consort now, and so of course they'd try to get on his good side. Vipers waiting to strike, more like.

"I remember you from the wedding," Hector said. It was his own little jab at them—they had been among those who stood for several seconds too long after they were meant to sit, as though they were considering walking out.

"How are you finding our beautiful Odentia, your Highness?" Lady Cassidy asked.

Hector internalized a sigh. It seemed like he would be stuck here for a while. "It's certainly a beautiful country. I'm fascinated by your right history. Though I've been studying quite diligently, there is always something new to learn."

"You must miss your home terribly," Lord Nathanial probed.

"I miss the family I left in Eldavon some, for sure," Hector said slowly. How would they use this against him? "However, I don't think it's fair to say that I miss home. Eldavon isn't my home anymore and hasn't been since the moment I married the queen. She is my home, and the family I dedicate myself to."

Nathanial and Cassidy glanced at each other with slightly wide eyes. Good. That took them by surprise. Hector nodded once more and turned to head back to the palace.

Of course, they weren't going to let him go that easily. Even as he stepped away, Lady Cassidy called out, "It's just such a shame. The place that used to be home must be a place you miss. It's a shame that you don't love this new home of yours."

Hector froze.

The people of Odentia knew well enough about a dragon's fated witch. Hector had had one, too. But he lost her, leaving him alone. He'd been so young, he couldn't say that he loved his fated mate, at least not in a romantic way. It stung all the same. In Eldavon, marriages were about love. You didn't marry someone you didn't love.

His marriage to Rowena, however, was purely for politics. He admired her greatly and already knew he got along with her before he agreed. It wasn't a simple decision, this arranged marriage, but neither was it forced on either of them. She chose him and he said yes.

That didn't mean there wasn't part of him that still pushed against the arrangement of it all. Part of him still mourned the love he might have found had he said no.

He turned on the Corellas, his hands clenching. "Is there a reason you're bothering me?" he snapped.

The two looked triumphant. Ah, so that's what it was. They wanted him to lose his patience, and now they got what they wanted. Hector ground his teeth together. Great. Now they'd be taking this story all through the court. Although, if he hadn't lost his patience, they could just make up something to say about him.

"Why, we're only making conversation," Lady Cassidy said.

"Perhaps, if you find such things as a simple discussion too difficult to deal with, you should recuse yourself from your duties as the Prince Consort," Lord Nathanial added. His faux friendliness slipped as he looked Hector up and down. "You have no business in our government."

Hector stepped forward but stopped when the two both flinched. It was that flinch more than their words that got to him. If they simply disliked him, that was one thing. But this... they were afraid of him. Just like the guards during the rebel attack.

He was here to help Odentia and Rowena. How was he meant to do that if they were all afraid of him?

"It's the queen's decision whether I am in the government or not," he said, keeping his voice flat. "Not yours or mine."

He didn't bother waiting around to see their reaction. He turned on his heel and marched back to Rowena's study. She had set aside her speech and was working on something else. When he entered, a brief, annoyed look crossed her face.

"I'm not changing this speech any further," she said firmly. "My head is going to explode if I try to work around everything. Some people will just have to be disappointed."

Hector opened his mouth then closed it again. What could he say, if she already made up her mind? There were all these accusations against him already. How much worse would they get if he started to be pushy about these things?

"Can I do anything to help you?" he finally asked.

Rowena shook her head.

"I'll leave you, then," he muttered, stepping back outside.

How much of a place did he actually have here? Had Rowena agreed to marry him just so she could get Odentia access to the Silver Springs? Was there a real marriage here, or was he just kidding himself?

His heart sank as he headed back to his rooms, the only place he could be guaranteed privacy. Apparently, he couldn't do as much good in Odentia as he initially believed.

CHAPTER
FIVE

Rowena checked her reflection in the mirror while her lady's maids hovered nearby to adjust any curl or fold of fabric that needed it. Her dark green dress swooped low on her bosom, though her cleavage was tastefully covered by gold lace. Golden suns trailed over her sleeves, which were fitted to her arms. The bust of her dress was tight; loose enough to breathe but fitted to show off her figure. The high waist of the skirt flowed to the floor and split down the middle to reveal a paler green underskirt.

"We will be waiting to help you remove the overdress as soon as you are done," Trella promised. She was the eldest of the lady's maids, and accustomed to what needed to be done to help the queen feel comfortable.

"Thank you," Rowena said. "I should have the crown now."

Trella lifted it to her head, securing it atop the elaborate braids and curls that had taken hours. Appearance was still very important as a queen, though Rowena refused to wear any jewelry other than the crown. She didn't want to appear over-bedecked.

She took a deep breath and then gestured for her lady's maids to open the door. She swept into the hall and toward the balcony where she would be making her appearance. The sun blazed overhead.

Rowena wished she could have worn a brimmed hat rather than the crown. She smiled as a cheer rose up from the plaza beneath her.

This balcony overlooked the street, where the people of the city gathered. She waved to them, to renewed cheers. The trumpets sounded, calling for silence, and she began.

"My people, today is a good day. I am pleased to announce that one hundred of our adults will be selected to journey to Eldavon's sacred Silver Springs and drink from the water, as I have done. Odentia will begin the process of receiving dragons and witches into our midst.

"Every adult on our census records will have the chance to be chosen," she continued, explaining her new selection plan. "There will be a lottery for every citizen of age. Whoever is chosen will have the opportunity to decline if they don't wish to go through the process. If they do choose to go, their needs, as well as the needs of their families, will be provided for by the Crown."

A burst of applause rang out. Rowena let out a silent sigh of relief. The means of selecting those to go to Eldavon had troubled her for some time until she came to this lottery.

She lifted her hands for quiet again. "You may be worried about whether dragons and witches from Odentia will know how to utilize their magic. We will be sending those who are revealed as dragons and witches through the Eldavon training, so they can then establish schools here in Odentia for future dragons and witches.

"Those of us who are humans of the Earth, we have an important role as well," she added. "This process will strengthen us all. Thank you for making this journey with me."

More cheering. Rowena waved to the crowd until it was time to retreat. She went back into the palace, the weight of the crown starting to become unbearable. The heat lingered on in her heavy overdress, soaking her through. Trella immediately set the maids removing it and the crown. Her underdress was just as modest as any regular day gown. The only thing that made it 'under' was the fact that it was worn under the heavier velvet.

Hector strode forward, bringing with him a glass of water. His silver eyes glowed as he grinned at her. They had decided that she would make this declaration alone, for fear that the people would be nervous at Hector's presence. Rowena hoped that they would find ways to be seen by the people together soon enough.

"You were wonderful." Hector handed her the water.

"Thank you." She drank, relieved to have the sweltering garment removed from her. "There's nothing else planned for our events today. Would you like to join me in the baths?"

Hector laughed. He went slightly pink as he nodded. "With how hot a day it is, I was hoping that we would be able to. Although," he added as they started toward the center of the palace, "your 'baths' here are much different from what I'm used to."

"Oh?"

"In my experience, what you call baths I'd call swimming pools," Hector explained. "I'd think of a bath as a small tub, just big enough to submerge most of the body in, that you use to scrub clean in."

Rowena's brow furrowed. "But I do clean in my bath."

"You clean and then rinse it off," Hector replied. "Rather than scrubbing off in the water. I daresay my method is more common. Most people don't have access to their own hot springs."

Rowena nodded. What he meant was a bath like the ones she took while on the road. Somehow it never occurred to her that that would be a person's normal, but he was right. Hot springs were fairly common in Odentia, yet not everyone would have access to one.

The palace had been built at a special convergence of a stream and springs. The three baths were built so that one had pure hot water, another just the stream, and the third a mix of the two. Each one was big enough to float in, with the coolest of the three deep and wide enough to swim laps in it.

Once at the baths, Rowena dismissed her lady's maids and stepped behind a privacy curtain to change into a black bodysuit made specifically for spending time in the water when she wasn't cleaning herself. She went back out and slipped into the coldest pool, shivering as the heat was sapped from her skin.

Hector came from his screen shortly after, also wearing a bodysuit. He dipped his foot into the cold pool and shook his head.

"Nope. Too cold." He instead lowered himself into the lukewarm pool.

"But that one isn't big enough to move around in," Rowena complained as she pushed herself through the water, warming herself up with movement.

Hector folded his arms to the side and rested his head on his arms.

"I forgot to thank you," he said, his expression earnest.

Rowena hesitated a moment, then pulled herself out of the cold pool to join him. The lukewarm water felt good on her now-cold skin. She settled into the wall, carved to have seats around the edge. "Thank me for what?"

"For taking into account the unfairness of the original plan," Hector said. "And thank you for listening to what I meant. I know I could have worded it better."

"You worded everything just fine. Honestly, I was most upset when you left before we finished talking about it," Rowena admitted, feeling a little awkward. She wasn't used to being so open with negative emotions.

Hector nodded, his brow furrowed in concentration. "I find that when I'm feeling argumentative about things that should be talked about, I need to take a break. Usually, it's because I'm feeling overstimulated and I need to have some time alone to recenter myself."

Rowena rested her head back against the side of the pool, careful to keep her hair out of the water. "And I can't recenter until things are taken care of."

Hector hummed. "We'll have to find a way for both of us to get what we need, then. Maybe if we remove ourselves to a new location to continue the discussion, or maybe if we have a specific length of time that we take a break?"

"That might work." Rowena turned, studying her husband. Her stomach fluttered as she considered the thing she'd been thinking about for the last few days.

On their trip here, they had shared a carriage and a tent. Since being back in the palace, they had been staying in separate chambers. Would Hector consider moving his things to her chambers? She had plenty of room for another bed to be moved into her rooms. It would allow them to be closer. Most married people lived together, didn't they?

As she started to formulate exactly how to word her request, though, the door opened. Trella came in, looking put out.

"Duke Volka is insisting that you come to the council chambers," Trella said. "There are, apparently, urgent matters regarding the lottery for the Silver Springs."

Rowena was tempted to duck beneath the water and pretend like she wasn't there. It was a childish impulse, one she quickly squashed. With a sigh, she got out of the water. Trella helped her to dry off and change back into her light under-dress. Once she had it on, the rest of the maids came in and put the stifling overdress back on her.

Hector was already changed and ready to go by the time she was done and they went to the council chambers together. There was an argument well underway by the time they got there. It didn't take long to figure out the problem. There were already reports coming in from the people unhappy about the proclamation.

"They seemed so pleased, though," Rowena said, stunned.

Volka shook his head. "They don't like that Eldavon will be training our people in their magic ways. The concern is that Odentia's customs will be erased for Eldavon's sake."

He shot a pointed look at Hector as he spoke.

Rowena closed her eyes, slumping back. They needed Eldavon to train their dragons and witches, as Odentia had no idea how. So how was she meant to proceed when people were so worried about Eldavon's influence?

It felt as though she was threading the tiniest of needles with invisible thread. How could she do it?

CHAPTER
SIX

Yet another official proclamation for the kingdom to hear. Hector adjusted the sleeves of the tight tunic he wore as he headed for Rowena's readying chambers. She was being prepared by her lady's maids so that she would look absolutely perfect when she stepped out on the balcony.

Hector's garb was much simpler; he was glad, because it meant he could ready himself. Though he should have a lord's man as Prince Consort, having someone waiting on him was even more uncomfortable than the clothing he wore. Being royalty had major drawbacks that he hadn't anticipated.

He shook those thoughts off, focusing instead on the moment. After careful consideration, Rowena had decided on another proclamation to assay the fears of Eldavon wiping out Odentia's traditions; this speech was to reassure the people that Odentia would remain Odentia and that the training that Eldavon would provide was the only way to learn how to use the powers that the Silver Springs bestowed on them.

Which was why this time, Hector would be with her, wearing the traditional Odentia clothing. For him, it was a tunic and trousers, all in black with silver moons embroidered on them. Even his hair was styled specifically, slicked back and held in place by a fruity-smelling oil of some sort. He would explain how the training process in Eldavon worked.

The clothes were strange and uncomfortable. It was tighter than he was used to, and without the special magic woven into it, these clothes would tear to pieces if he shifted. But it looked good, he had to admit that. The clothes emphasized the width of his shoulders and cut a striking figure. Even the boots with their slightly raised heel made him taller.

With everything that was happening, a little discomfort was worth it. This was the most visually obvious thing to show he was embracing Odentia traditions.

He'd get used to the feel of them in time. Besides this, he had already commissioned various new clothes in the Odentia style to be made for him, which he could send to Eldavon to receive the spells that would allow them to survive the shift between forms.

He stopped outside of the ready room, folding his hands behind his back as he leaned against the wall. A smile spread over his face as he considered the last few days.

It had been stressful, yes, but at the same time, he had been able to see Rowena more in her element. She was focused, dedicated, and sure of herself. They had had arguments over what the best course of action was, but even those disagreements remained calm. She really was an amazing woman, and he was glad it was her, and not someone else, who ended up as Odentia's ruler.

As he stood there, waiting, the sound of voices came out to him. The door had been left open a sliver. Hector reached to close it, but the sound of his name stopped him.

"Hector is a very handsome man indeed," said the voice. "I trust your marriage is... pleasant?"

Hector flushed. Was that one of Rowena's maids?

"My husband is very handsome and my marriage pleasant," Rowena answered, sounding cool. "Lady Devonna, is there a reason you have decided to come speak with me at this time?"

Ah, Lady Devonna. She was part of Rowena's court, one of her ladies-in-waiting. Hector still wasn't entirely clear as to what a lady-in-waiting did, other than spend time with the queen.

"I was just wanting to speak with you about that ball you plan to host, the one introducing him as Prince Consort," Devonna hedged.

The one in which Hector would make his pledges to Rowena, to serve her as his queen. They were pledges that he was more than happy to take. But what was Devonna bringing them up for?

"Forgive me, your Majesty," Devonna continued, lowering her voice. Hector had to lean closer to the door to hear her. "I'm just… Well, I would like to think that I'm one of the people in the palace who can speak plainly to you."

Rowena sighed. "Then speak plainly."

Devonna was quiet a moment longer before speaking in a rush. "I'm just uncertain as to what role he really plays here. In the palace, but also as your husband. He is a handsome man and has an easy nature about him. The times that I have interacted with the man, he seems to be most amiable indeed. A gentle, good man."

Well, that was better than being afraid of him. Hector's chest tightened all the same. If even the people who were on his side questioned his role here in Odentia, what chance did he have to win over those who were against him?

This wasn't the sort of life he had envisioned for himself here. He thought, perhaps naively, that it would be… simpler. That the opposition would be more obvious.

"Don't be angry with me, your Majesty. I'm only saying what I see." Devonna sighed. "He knows so little about Odentia. I know he's from an influential family, but he's not nobility. He doesn't understand how things are here."

"I'm teaching him what needs to be done," Rowena answered.

"Of course," Devonna answered.

Perhaps her expression said more than she did because Rowena continued. "As for the details of my marriage, that need not concern you. I'm happy with my husband, and that's all there is to it. He is a good man, which is why I chose him."

"Yes. That is not in question," Devonna said carefully.

"I married him because Odentia needed the connection to Eldavon," Rowena said, sounding almost as though she was talking to herself. "He expects nothing else from our union and neither do I. This is both for the sake of our current peace and future flourishment."

Hector winced and moved to the other side of the hallway. *This is why you don't eavesdrop,* he scolded himself. *What else do you expect when you go around listening to people's private conversations?*

His shoulders slumped as he sagged against the wall. Nothing Rowena had just said was untrue. He agreed with everything she had just said—those were all the reasons he agreed to this marriage. Because while political matches weren't a thing in Eldavon, they made a lot of sense in Odentia.

He went into this marriage knowing it would be nothing but a political match. He thought that would be enough... but things were changing. For him, at least. When he thought of Rowena, his heart fluttered. When he wasn't with her, he longed to be with her. He wanted to see her laugh and smile, wanted to be there to comfort and bolster her.

It was clear from Rowena's conversation with Devonna that her feelings weren't the same. She still viewed their match through a pragmatic lens.

It made sense. She needed to put her kingdom first; besides, she couldn't make herself love him any more than he could stop himself from loving her. He'd just have to accept that his feelings were different from hers.

He inhaled deeply, steadying himself. Then, squaring his shoulders, he marched back over to the door and knocked.

"Rowena?" he called. "It's time."

CHAPTER

SEVEN

Once they clarified things, the reports grew much more positive. Rowena felt as though she was stressed all the time, but at least things were progressing. She was very busy with all of the selections and making sure that the right people were contacted. It was all very intensive. Rowena found that all she wanted to do at the end of the day was float in her baths, utterly alone.

Well... with Hector. He offered her more silent support than she had ever expected. She wasn't sure how she would manage without him.

Within the next few weeks, the people selected via lottery were all gathered together at the palace. Out of the hundred originally chosen, fourteen refused to come. Rowena met them all personally to thank them for their trust in her. She was shocked to see what a state some of them were in. Even though new clothes were provided, many were clearly malnourished and acted as though simple shoes were the greatest blessing they had.

"I never realized how much a difference there was between my life and my people's," she told Hector the morning they were to see off the people to Eldavon. "I should have investigated my own people's conditions much more thoroughly than I have."

"You have had a lot to deal with," Hector pointed out.

Rowena shook her head. "But this just comes back to what you told me, about there being too much stratification between the nobility and the workers we rely on. I didn't take you as seriously as I should have. I've been so wrapped up in my own troubles."

Hector smoothed her hair from her cheek and smiled at her. Her heart started beating faster; was he going to kiss her?

To her disappointment, he lowered his hand again. "So, what are you going to do about it?"

"I'm going to ask you to step into the role that would normally be occupied by a king's wife," she told him, smiling wryly. "Organize charitable drives and funds to lift the poorest of Odentia out of poverty. I don't see how my duties will give me enough time to do the arrangements myself."

Hector's smile only widened. "You think that it'll make people like me more?"

Rowena flushed, biting her lip. "That's part of the hope, yes."

"I'd be honored," Hector said, growing serious once more.

Relief washed through her. She knew that Eldavon wasn't as stringent with their roles as Odentia was, but she had still worried Hector would find the request beneath him. She ought to have known better—he was the kindest person she knew, so of course he would want to help people.

"I suppose we should go out and see them," Rowena said, turning her mind to the current situation.

The people selected to go to Eldavon were ready to start their journey. It was a massive caravan that would take them to the Eldavon palace, with many wagons to carry all the people and what possessions they were taking with them.

Hector nodded once. "Remind me what I'm supposed to do again? Stand behind you and try not to look scary?"

Rowena laughed as she looped her arm through his. "Stand next to me and laugh at all my jokes is more like it."

He obliged with a chuckle.

They headed out together, the guards falling in behind them once they left the chambers. The caravan oxen snorted impatiently as people milled about. Many of those who were going were hugging those being left behind. Plenty of tears were being shed. Though Rowena's heart clenched to see these goodbyes, she knew it was the best for everyone.

She walked among them for a time, talking quietly. The people she greeted gave her nervous bows and curtsies. Rowena breathed deeply through her own nerves, feeling herself grounding more firmly to the earth beneath her feet. This would be a good thing, for all of them.

When all was ready, she mounted her horse and led the caravan as it started out. Hector rode slightly behind her, watchful. His normal jovial expression was serious, though the way his eyes turned up at the edges still made him look like he was smiling. The two of them leading the caravan was merely a symbolic gesture; they would turn back in time to return to the palace before dark.

As they rode, though, Rowena wished that decorum would allow him to come right beside her. "It's so difficult to talk to you like this," she said without turning; it wouldn't be proper for her to be continually twisting around.

"I thought that we weren't meant to do a lot of talking during this procession," Hector replied. He sounded too serious for it to be a joke; he'd been more serious quite often of late. It was as though he finally understood the gravity of their situation, perhaps.

Rowena didn't like it. He was especially dashing in the black and silver uniform he had commissioned, but he never looked more handsome than when he was joking and laughing. Lately, even his smiles seemed to be forced. Had she done something wrong? Or was it the stress of the situation?

Perhaps when they got back home, they would be able to have some more time to talk this through. Whatever was happening, she wouldn't find any relief until she was able to hear the problem plainly. This wasn't a situation where she needed to let him recenter before she pressed, was it? If it was, then he needed to tell her.

No. Most likely it was going to be the caravan situation. She just had to be certain of it.

She inhaled through her nose, calming herself once more. She reached out through her senses, embracing the solidity around her. Whatever had happened, they would sort through it. She wasn't granted the powers of the Earth for nothing. As the people of Eldavon told her, she was a balancing force—and she would see it through.

Her mind was so swept up by Hector and the problems they might be facing that the attack came out of nowhere. One moment she was drawing strength into her convictions, and the next, there was screaming.

Her horse bucked, whinnying as its ears pinned back to its skull. The sounds of metal clashed as armored rebels went for the guards. A handful of them slipped around the guards and raced for her. One of them grabbed her horse's reins and yanked hard, pulling the horse back to the ground. Screams rose from the caravan.

Rowena kicked out, her foot colliding with the rebel's head. The man stumbled back, dragging the horse in a circle. Another of the rebels grabbed her arm. She yelped as he dragged her from her horse. She shoved at the man but his grip was too tight.

A fist flew out of nowhere, smashing the rebel in the face. Hector wrapped his arms around her, spinning away from the other rebels. Red scales sprang to life along his exposed skin. Rowena yanked at her heavy skirt, trying to rip it free; she couldn't fight alongside him if she was weighed down by these clothes!

A woman sidestepped through the guards and flung a knife at Rowena. It spiraled toward her and Hector threw himself in the way. The blade sliced through his shoulder. He roared as his wings snapped out, shredding the back of his uniform.

Rowena's heart hammered. Her gaze locked onto the place where he'd been cut. Her mouth opened but she had no air to speak as the scales around the area started to disappear. She knew what was happening, even in the blur of activity. The blade had been poisoned. Emerald Rattleback venom, which prevented a dragon from shifting—

The blade!

Rowena lunged for it as Hector's wings disappeared. She snatched it up and cut away the overskirt she wore. The soldiers gathered around her, forming a tight ring as they fought against the rebels. Hector was jostled out of the ring.

"Wait," she cried as the guards started herding her toward the wagons, which had circled into a protective barrier. "Hector!"

He blocked a rebel that swung at him and with a smooth movement, disarmed the woman. Then he used the sword against the others, seemingly unhampered by his injuries.

"To the queen," one of the guards shouted. "We must protect the queen!"

The people selected to go to the Silver Springs were driven here and there by the rebels. Swords waved and people screamed. The sounds roared in Rowena's ears as she gripped the dagger tightly. She tried to get free of her guards, to help the people.

"Stop," Rowena whispered. She tried to find that power in herself she had felt before, that grounding, balancing power.

But all she could feel was the chaos as the rebels continued their attack.

CHAPTER
EIGHT

"Give it up, dragon!" the man spat at Hector, swinging his sword at his head. "You can't shift, you're helpless!"

Hector ignored the taunt. He blocked the sword and spun around, twisting his blade down to slice the man's arm. The rebel howled as the sword dropped from his hand. He turned to run but was tripped by a guard, who dropped on him and twisted his arms behind his back.

Another rebel was holding off several guards and Hector raced over to help. He flipped a second sword into his free hand and with the dual blades, distracted the rebel long enough that one of the guards was able to club him over the head. All around them, the rebels were either fleeing or surrendering. Hector glanced toward the line of bodies being lined up near one of the caravan wagons.

Most of these rebels were poorly armored and could barely use a weapon, so many of them didn't survive the attack. Those who were injured, not killed, were thankfully higher on both sides. Hector hurried to find Rowena. She'd removed her outer gown entirely, free in her high-waisted underdress. She was already working on helping to bind injuries.

"Are you alright?" Hector asked as he came to her.

She nodded once, not looking away from her work. "Are you?"

"Yes. I'm going to go help find the people who were driven into the forest."

Rowena finished tying a knot and looked up at him with concerned eyes. She opened her mouth, then shut it again and swallowed.

What was she going to say? Hector hesitated, but there was still too much work to be done. He headed off once more. Those who had been selected to go the Silver Springs had largely stayed within the wagons, but some of them had fled when the fighting started. Hector went with a handful of guards, careful not to let his guard down.

Soon, they came across a group of travelers as they limped in circles, clearly lost.

"It's alright," Hector said soothingly, lifting his hands. "We'll show you back to the caravan. The attack is over."

One of them, a grey-haired woman leaning on a younger man for support, glared at him. "And what were you doing? What's the point of having a dragon in our kingdom if you're just going to hide away until the fighting is over."

"Hey," one of the guards snapped. "His Royal Highness was fighting alongside us!"

"I didn't see no dragon," the woman insisted.

Hector winced. "I would have taken my dragon form, but I was prevented. See this?"

He showed his shoulder. Now that the adrenaline was wearing off, he realized he should have had it dressed. It stung terribly and the venom working through his system was making him feel chilled. It wouldn't kill him, though.

"I was cut by a blade that had Emerald Rattleback venom on it. If a dragon gets that venom into their system, we can't shift anymore." He shook his head. "It seemed the rebels were prepared for me."

The young man gasped. "But I thought dragons were invincible!"

Hector shook his head. "We contain sun magic, and so we have perhaps the most obvious magic, but we are hardly invincible."

"But you are the most powerful," the young man insisted.

37

"No. Only the most obvious," Hector repeated. He held out a hand toward them. "Let's get back to the caravan. I can help you walk."

The woman gave him a distrustful look, but with a grunt, accepted his hand. It soon became clear that she injured her leg in her flight, and Hector carried her bridal style in his arms. She grumbled, pink-faced, the entire time. When they got back to the caravan, Rowena made Hector sit down so she could tend to his shoulder.

"I want to go home," said one of the selected people, a young woman with tears running down her face. "I don't want to do this anymore."

Hector glanced at Rowena, checking if she had heard. Her expression was troubled; her gaze flickered up to him. Despite the unsettling nature of the events that happened, there was a firmness to her eyes, a steadiness that took Hector's breath away.

She took a deep breath as she cleaned out the cut. "How long will the venom affect you?"

"Not too much longer," Hector answered. "It's only a small cut."

Rowena nodded. She wrapped clean bandages around his shoulder. "You should avoid using it for a while. Will you want to speak with the rebels?"

"Yes. I think it's best if I do," Hector answered.

"Then you should go." Rowena collected her things and turned toward the young woman. Hector sat as she knelt beside the woman and asked to check the woman's injured arm. The woman's eyes were huge as she held it out.

"I know this is a terrifying thing to happen," Rowena said, starting to work. "And if you wish to return to your home, you may. There will be no repercussions and you will have the chance to go to the Springs in the future. But please let me say a few reasons why it will be best to continue."

Hector stood stiffly. While Rowena calmly reassured the people, he headed toward the wagon where the rebels were bound. The guards nodded at him with a newfound respect in their eyes; apparently, the way he'd fought hand-to-hand had impressed them.

"Which one is their leader?" he asked their captain of the guard, Hugo.

"That one." Hugo pointed at a man with a bloody bandage on his forehead.

Hector faced the rebel, frowning. "What was the point of this?"

The rebel glared at him. "We are protecting our kingdom from the likes of you!"

"So all this just to kill me?" Hector lifted an eyebrow. "It seems to me that you hurt your own people far more than me. How could it be worth it to be so brazen when an assassin would do the job with less damage to your kingdom? No. You were coming for the queen."

Hugo growled, putting a hand on the hilt of his sword.

The rebel lifted himself up, sneering. "Once you're dead, she will have no power. She'll have no choice but to bring Prince Finnegan back from his exile. He should be king!"

Hector bit back a groan. "Finnegan isn't exiled. He can't return because of a spell—"

"Spells that you put on him!" one of the other rebels yelled. "If the child-queen had any strength, she would have forced Eldavon to return him."

Child-queen? Finnegan was barely older than Rowena was! She was an adult and a married woman. How could they possibly consider her a child?

The rebel leader glared at him. "We will say no more."

"Why do you think Finnegan would make a better ruler than Rowena?" Hector asked.

But true to his word, the leader was silent. Hector couldn't get any of them to speak after that, and so stepped back from the interrogation —there was still a lot of other things to be done. He returned to Rowena and helped her. Once the injuries were all taken care of, the caravan was turned back to the palace; they would need to delay the journey.

"What shall we do with the prisoners?" Hugo asked once they were on the move again.

Unlike before, Rowena and Hector were both in a wagon this time. It wasn't just because of the fear of a new attack, but their state of dress—or undress. Hector's tunic had been torn to uselessness when he was trying to shift, and Rowena's overdress was beyond repair as well. Though Hector was given a fresh shirt and they were both perfectly decent in his eyes, it was an unwritten rule that they couldn't be seen like this.

"I want them all sent to the prison," Rowena answered Hugo. "They will be kept locked up until their trials."

"Trials," Hector repeated. "And then what?"

Rowena folded her arms. "Treason has always been dealt with harshly."

A prickling ran down Hector's spine. She didn't mean execution, did she? "They might be able to be reasoned with."

"If they attacked us once, they'll do it again. Why should I let them go free when they're trying to overthrow me?" Rowena snapped at him. Her shoulders hunched further. "But of course you won't understand. Nobody from Eldavon could possibly understand."

Hector drew back. He opened his mouth, but the only words that wanted to come were just as bitter as the ones Rowena had just said.

So, he turned his face away from her and was silent.

Rowena sighed. "Hector…"

He waited.

"I didn't mean… I just…" She fell silent again.

The tension remained between them as they returned to the palace. Once there, Hector went to his chambers. He dropped onto his bed, staring up at the ceiling as he turned the events of the day over in his mind. Part of him wanted to go to Rowena and hash this out, but what was there to hash out?

She married him for the connections to Eldavon.

But it seemed that she, just like everyone else, would never see him as belonging here.

He wasn't sure how long he was in there before a knock came at the door. When he answered it, Hugo stood on the other side, looking exhausted and furious.

"We've gotten word from Eldavon," Hugo said, handing him a piece of paper. "Several of their villages have been raided. By people bringing the Odentia banner with them."

CHAPTER
NINE

Hector's face was grim as he and Hugo stepped into Rowena's study. She hadn't been there more than half an hour, sorting through everything that had happened. When Hugo delivered the news, her heart sank.

Rowena covered her face with her hands. Her head pounded as she tried to think clearly. It was obvious that these attacks had been timed to be close to when they were meant to start sending people to Eldavon, perfectly coordinated for the news to arrive right at this moment.

"Your orders, Your Majesty?" Hugo asked grimly.

Rowena drew herself back up, stiffening her spine so she would not slump. "Send soldiers to find the people using our banner and stop them."

Hugo bowed to her smartly and left the study.

"I don't know why he told you first instead of me," Rowena muttered as she slumped back into her chair.

"He thought I'd be able to contact the palace in Eldavon and warn them," Hector answered.

Rowena looked at him hopefully.

He grimaced and shook his head. "The Rattleback venom is still stopping me from being able to access my magic."

"Then I can only hope that the kings and queens of Eldavon don't think that I've decided to attack them and that I've done something to you to prevent you from being able to contact them," Rowena said bitterly.

Now that Silas was gone, they were supposed to get back to normal. Yes, there were always going to be hiccups, but she had, naively, thought that once she got things going, she'd be able to have forward momentum. Now, it felt like everything was backsliding. No matter how hard she clawed at the side of the mountain, she couldn't find purchase to stop.

Hector shook his head. "After everything you've done to build peace? Our kings and queens aren't hasty in their judgments; we all know about the rebels. They won't assume anything, and once the venom wears off, I'll be able to contact the court and inform them of this attack as well."

Rowena gave him a pained smile. "I bet you're wishing that your cousin Kaia was here now. So she could be helping with all of this."

"We agreed that I needed to be the only one around for a while until people got used to a dragon's presence," Hector answered.

"How long until the venom wears off?"

Hector hummed as he swung his arm in a circle, more vigorously than Rowena liked considering he'd been injured. "It's difficult to tell. It seems to have been a concentrated dose. I should be able to get through to them by tomorrow morning at least."

Rowena glanced through one of her narrow windows, shocked to see it was growing dark outside. She must have been in here much longer than she realized. Her stomach rumbled. It was time to get something to eat—and drink if the tension headache she was becoming aware of was any indication.

She sighed. It would be far easier to use the Gorgon mirrors to contact Eldavon, but they couldn't due to Silas's influence. There was much work to be done with them before anyone grew comfortable using them regularly.

Hector glanced at her stomach and Rowena blushed. Had he heard the unseemly noises that it made? He grinned at her, a wide, warm smile that lessened some of the tension in her shoulders.

"Why don't we take dinner in my chambers?" he asked, offering her his hand. "We can talk about what we need to do next while we eat."

Rowena nodded reluctantly. She had been in here all day and wasn't any closer to figuring out what to do. So what was the harm of a change of scenery? As she and Hector started toward his chambers, waves of exhaustion rolled over her. She found herself fantasizing about Hector sweeping her into his arms and carrying her to his room, where he would tuck her into bed and bring her food and water, then sit with her until she fell asleep.

They were quiet during their food. Rowena attempted to force some conversation, but her mind was so full of other things that she couldn't concentrate on Hector's replies.

After she'd eaten and night had truly fallen, Rowena sighed. She glanced around Hector's chambers. They were wide and ornate, just as everything in the palace was. Nothing in the room spoke to Hector personally, other than the portraits of his huge family hanging on the walls.

"You should probably get to your chambers," Hector told her. "Try to get some rest."

The idea of being by herself made Rowena shudder. "Can I sleep here?"

Hector's eyes widened.

Heat crept up Rowena's cheeks but she returned his gaze steadily. "We're married, so it's not odd. We shared a bed while we were traveling here during our honeymoon. And I felt so much comfort, listening to you breathe next to me. I don't want to be alone tonight."

"Then... yes. Of course, you can stay," Hector said. There was a strange pinch to his brow.

Rowena didn't bother to spend much time trying to decipher it. She ordered for her sleeping clothes to be brought to Hector's room, and dismissed her lady's maids to get ready for bed herself. Part of her wondered if she should feel more giddy to once more share a bed with her husband, but she was so dead tired that she couldn't even think of such things.

It wasn't a restful night, but she did sleep some. The bed was so large that she and Hector didn't even share blankets, but just having him close by was a comfort.

In the morning, Hector already had breakfast brought to the room when she woke up. Rowena fell on the food ravenously, as though she hadn't eaten in a week.

"I was able to contact Eldavon this morning," he told her. "I explained everything that's happened. And as expected, nobody thinks that this is your doing."

Rowena picked up her tea and sipped at it, satisfied after such a large meal. Despite that, her stomach squeezed, a sudden queasiness coursing through her. The taste of the tea turned rancid in her mouth and she had to set it aside.

"That's good," she said slowly. "But there is something else that I need to ask of you."

Hector's brow pinched. "What is it?"

"I decided something last night—something I know is a risk," she said, her hands twisting in her lap. "I want you to fly me out to the border so that I can speak with the rebels there myself."

She bit her lip, watching Hector closely for his reaction. Emotions flitted over his face, shifting rapidly as he processed what she was saying. Eventually, his mouth set into a thin line as he folded his arms and narrowed his eyes at her.

"No."

"I know it's a risk—"

"It's more than a risk, it's unnecessary," Hector said. "We have no idea what their true motivations are. I'm not going to be part of you getting yourself killed."

Rowena shook her head. "I've thought this through. I need to show my hand here; I need to prove that I am capable of rising to these challenges. And I know in my bones that this is what I need to do."

Hector shook his head stubbornly. "I know that you only married me because you needed connections to Eldavon. I know that I don't really have a place here—"

"What makes you say—" Rowena started.

"I heard you talking with Lady Devonna." His arms tightened.

Rowena's eyes widened. "You heard—"

"I don't understand the intricacies of Odentia society. I know that. But I came here with a purpose and I'm going to do the best I can," Hector continued, glaring at her now. "Taking you somewhere where you will get killed is against everything I swore to do as your husband."

"But that's just the thing. I don't think they'll hurt me," Rowena interjected.

Hector shook his head. "You have no way of knowing that."

"No, but I have to be able to trust myself. Isn't that what the Silver Springs is about?" Rowena asked desperately. "I'll admit, it sounds crazy. But when I said I felt as though the springs changed me, I meant it. It's like I can feel the Earth beneath me, turning me toward the border and moving me there. I can't explain it, other than to say that I need to do this."

"And if you're wrong?"

Rowena hesitated. When she thought of this plan, it seemed the best course of action. Now as she stared into his silver eyes, she realized she wasn't just putting herself at risk, but him as well. Could she really risk him?

Hector closed his eyes. "I know you chose me for a reason. And I accepted for that same reason. But things have changed—for me at least." He bowed his head like he couldn't bear to look at her. "I've come to love you, Rowena. I love you—I can't lose you."

All the air left her lungs. A thrill shot through her and her mouth opened slightly. No words came out, though she felt like singing. Love. He loved her.

"Hector..."

CHAPTER
TEN

Hector looked up at Rowena saying his name so softly. He held his breath as he gazed into her dark brown eyes. Her hands twined tightly in her lap and her cheeks were rosy. She started to lean forward, lifting one of her hands as though to cup his face in her hand.

The doors to his chambers burst open. Rowena jumped and Hector leapt to his feet, already putting himself between her and whoever was coming in. It wasn't rebels or attackers, though. Rather, it was Duke Volka and Lord Corella. Nathaniel Corella looked smug as he sauntered in after the duke.

"What do you think you're doing?" Hector snarled. "You can't just barge into my chambers like this!"

"We require the queen," Volka answered.

The flames of Hector's dragon flickered in his chest. He wanted nothing more than to yell at the two lords but forced himself to swallow his anger. He would not give them further ammunition to use against him. They were the ones acting rudely, and though they might deserve rudeness in return, Hector wanted to show he was above that.

"You require the queen, so you simply let yourselves into our private space?" Hector continued to stand in front of Rowena as she

47

wrapped herself in a blanket. "You will leave. When we have dressed, we will come to the council chambers, where you will apologize to the queen."

"There's no—" Nathaniel started.

Hector lifted his hand. "You will apologize to the queen. Now leave my chambers."

Volka's gaze flickered to Rowena before he averted his eyes. He bowed deeply. "Of course. We will wait in the council chambers."

Nathanial scowled, but followed Volka out.

Rowena cast off the blanket and grabbed the fresh dress that had been left with breakfast. Hector opened his mouth but she scurried back into the bedroom to change out of her nightdress. He groaned as he sank back to the couch. It was clear that whatever she had been planning on saying to him was lost.

But what had she planned to say? If the conversation he'd overheard was any indication, she didn't feel the same way about him as he did about her. It made his heart ache, but he would accept it—one couldn't change how they felt so easily. But he really did hate how this moment had been interrupted.

After Rowena returned, he went to his bedroom to change out of his sleeping clothes as well. He chose his Eldavon uniform, wanting to be sure that he could shift to this dragon form if necessary.

Rowena gave him a sweeping glance when he joined her but didn't comment on his clothes. She was silent as they went to the council chambers, where all the advisors had already gathered. They appeared to be in the middle of an argument already.

"Your Majesty," Volka said loudly, quieting the others. "I must apologize for disturbing you so early in the morning."

Hector narrowed his eyes—that wasn't exactly the apology he needed to make.

Rowena took her seat at the table. "Next time, you will send a servant before you decide to disturb my privacy, Duke," she said, her voice hard. "Especially when I am alone with my husband. Now what is so urgent?"

Volka bowed his head slightly toward her. "It's this matter of sending our people to Eldavon. I believe you should postpone the exchange until these rebellions are dealt with."

Nathanial snorted. "They should be canceled altogether! Nobody wants it to happen."

Hector glared at him, biting his tongue. If he was from Odentia, he'd have plenty to say as Prince Consort. But here as a dragon and with Rowena's authority already so tenuous, he couldn't freely express himself.

"It's quite rude to call me 'nobody,' Lord Corella," Rowena answered. Though her tone was even, her expression was hard. Her hands clenched under the table.

How long would it be before she lost her temper entirely with these people? Once more, Hector had to bite back the desire to stand up for her. They were meant to be her advisors, but from what Hector saw, these men acted more like bullies. Even those who occasionally were on her side, like Volka, clearly didn't respect her as a ruler.

"I talked with many of the people who were selected to go yesterday, once we returned to the palace," Rowena continued. "Whoever is still willing to go will go."

"And I agree," Volka quickly said, nodding.

Corella scowled at them both.

"My concern is that the rebels will continue to act out and endanger the entire project," Volka continued. "Which is why I suggest postponing the exchange. Things are moving very quickly. Perhaps too quickly, your Majesty. I admire your concern for the kingdom, but perhaps more caution is warranted."

More caution. Like not flying out to the border to talk with the rebels with only a single dragon for protection. Hector shifted uncomfortably on the spot. Perhaps Volka had a point after all.

"I understand your concerns," Rowena said slowly. "But this process will already take years."

"Better to have delays than to risk our people," Volka said softly.

Hector cleared his throat. "Perhaps I can be of use here?" He glanced at Rowena, who nodded at him. She was twisting the hems of her sleeves now, clearly struggling to hide how nervous she was.

Hector straightened himself as he continued, "I contacted the Eldavon palace dragons mind-to-mind this morning already. I can do it again, and be a conduit for a more detailed discussion between our kingdoms."

Corella gave him a look of sheer poison.

"It might even be possible for some dragons and witches to fly out here, to help escort the caravan to Eldavon," he offered. "This exchange is deeply important to Eldavon as well."

Corella jumped to his feet. "We don't need any more of your interference! We are Odentian. We don't need to become like you!"

"Sit down," Volka snapped.

"Don't you see?" Corella threw his hands into the air. "They're trying to annex us!"

Volka turned on him, but it was Rowena who spoke. "Sit. Down."

Corella opened his mouth, glaring at her.

"Hugo," Rowena said, turning toward the guard. "Remove Lord Corella from these chambers."

"What?" Corella yelped.

"Take him to his chambers and post a guard," Rowena continued. "He will remain there and think about how he might better learn to contain himself in these meetings."

Hugo marched over to Corella, who blustered as he stared at Rowena.

Hector had to fight a grin. He'd never seen a grown man grounded before! Corella snarled under his breath as Hugo escorted him out.

Rowena took a deep breath and released it slowly.

"Now that that's over." She turned to Hector. "I may ask you to contact Eldavon like you've suggested. For now, though, I want you to go talk with the people selected by the lottery. I want to have a better idea of what they want before I make any decisions."

Surprise rippled through him. Hector slowly got to his feet, fighting against the feelings of disappointment that swept through him. It was perfectly logical for Rowena to send him to talk to them. After all, he was the one who could best answer any questions they had about the process itself.

But it still stung. It still felt as though he was being carefully removed from the council chambers... because he was a dragon. Because he wasn't from Odentia.

Because as much as Rowena wanted him for his ties to Eldavon... maybe he really didn't belong here after all.

CHAPTER
ELEVEN

By the time she was done meeting with her advisors, Rowena felt as though she had been wrung through the laundry. Every inch of her ached, especially her feet for some reason—her shoes felt oddly tight even though she had been sitting the whole time. Maybe that was why; she was used to moving more than this, and the chairs weren't exactly comfortable.

The only thing that had been decided absolutely was that the guard for the caravan would be doubled on the way to Eldavon. She was not going to delay this anymore than was absolutely necessary. The connections with Eldavon were only a part of it—having magic in their lives would also make Odentia far better.

It was nighttime before she was able to see Hector again. She invited him to her chambers this time. He came, bringing with him a wrapped parcel.

"Were you able to talk to the selected people?" Rowena asked him. It was the last thing she wanted to ask, but it was the most important.

"Yes. It seems like most are still willing to see this through." Hector set the package on the coffee table and took an armchair, though she had left plenty of space on the couch with her. "Do you still want to fly out to speak with the rebels?"

There was a sharp edge to his voice. Rowena's shoulders slumped. "No. I still think we should have this morning, but the moment has passed. Something changed. Or maybe I really wasn't thinking clearly this morning."

Hector's mouth pinched tight.

"Don't look at me like that. King Sydney and Queen Abigail said something about being human before we left. They told me that the thing I needed to be most aware of is that Earth magic gives us strong feelings, convictions. We need to trust ourselves and our instincts, sometimes even over common sense."

Hector ran his hand through his brown hair. "I... wish I could say that I don't question that. I clearly haven't learned enough about what it means to be human. Even in Eldavon, where we always say that humans, dragons, and witches are equal, there is more importance placed on the latter two."

Rowena laced her fingers together, staring at her hands. "I expect people to question me. I expect them to think that I'm not capable of making the right choices. It's what I have faced my entire life. I need your support, Hector. Even when you disagree with me."

"I can't do anything that will put you in danger."

Her heart skipped a beat. The reasons why he couldn't hung between them, spoken once and now silently looming over them. It would be so easy to reach over to him and say she knew exactly how he felt—

But the kingdom came first.

Rowena inhaled deeply, calming the swirling emotions running through her. They would have time later. Time to give this discussion the weight it deserved.

"I need to talk with Eldavon," she said, lifting her head again.

The disappointment in his eyes made her stomach pang.

"Of course." He picked up the package. "When I was in contact with the palace earlier, they told me that the corruption in the Gorgon mirrors has all been cleared and they're safe to use for communication. Travel is still uncertain for the time being."

He opened the package, revealing an obsidian-framed mirror on the inside. The sight of it made Rowena draw back. Memories of the fog she was lost in when Silas initially took her prisoner turned her skin cold. But she trusted Hector's words.

Soon, she held the mirror in her hands and gazed in. Rather than seeing herself reflected, the image of Queen Johanna, Eldavon's witch queen, was framed in the mirror.

"I'm glad to see that you're alright," Johanna said. "We have sent people to deal with the situation on our border. We have already collected a handful of the attackers and are pursuing the rest to find their camps."

Rowena nodded. That would be why her presence couldn't make a difference now. The rebels, once confronted by dragons and Eldavon soldiers, wouldn't be willing to listen to her. She repressed the urge to tell Johanna about her feelings from this morning, to see if the other queen would agree with her or Hector.

"Thank you," she said instead. She could have insisted and argued with Hector more. Instead, she had let her advisors pull her into those endless arguments. Speaking of what they were arguing about... "Things aren't faring much better here. While it appears most of the people selected still want to go to Eldavon, there is a growing discontent about our arrangement."

Johanna tucked a piece of hair behind her ear. "What sort of discontent are we talking about?"

Rowena closed her eyes briefly. "There've been several organized protests in the merchant districts, calling for the magic to be made illegal entirely here in Odentia. City guards had to stop quite a few skirmishes."

"It seems that the rebels organized more than just attacking the caravan," Hector added.

"I can't assume that they're all rebels," Rowena said, shaking her head. "Even with our attempts to share the truth, there's a lot of misunderstanding of what this means for Odentia. We have to make more effort into combating that misinformation."

"That is wise," Johanna agreed. "Most times these things come from a base of fear. The best way to reassure people is to share the truth with them."

Rowena nodded.

"How will we do it?" Hector asked.

"We'll have to come up with a plan," Rowena hedged.

In truth, she had no idea. She thought that they had already done a good job at sharing exactly what this program meant and how it would benefit Odentia. If Finnegan were here, maybe he would be able to tell her exactly what to do. But he wasn't here… though now with the mirrors…

"Can I speak with my uncle?" she asked hopefully.

Johanna grimaced. "I will make sure to arrange a time for you to speak with him. Unfortunately, right now I have too much going on to take the time to be flown to the top of Mount Eldavon. I'm sorry."

"Of course." She had to figure this out on her own, trusting her own instincts.

She and Johanna discussed the situation for a while longer and agreed that a handful of dragon-witch pairs would fly out to join the caravan closer to the Eldavon border, in case more of the rebels were waiting in Odentia to ambush them. Those in Eldavon would be imprisoned until arrangements could be made to send them to the capitol.

After they were done talking, Rowena wrapped up the mirror again and slumped into the couch. "I want the people who organized the protests to be brought to the palace; and a good selection of the protestors, too. Ones who aren't leaders but are still involved."

Hector frowned.

"I'll write them invitations myself," she decided, turning her gaze to stare at the ceiling. "I need to talk with them."

"You could be inviting assassins right into your parlor."

Rowena nodded, still not looking at him. "I could be. But one of the things I loved about Eldavon was that your kings and queens weren't held above the people. They were still citizens of your kingdom. Every job was counted just as vital as a ruler."

Hector hummed. "And you want to break down some of the social hierarchy here in Odentia?"

Rowena pushed herself to sit up straight again. "Exactly. If I'm going to change things for my people, it won't be without risk. I can't let my own fears stop me from doing what's best for the kingdom. For my people."

"I... suppose that's true," Hector agreed.

"It is. I can see now how much desperate poverty my people suffer. I can see how so many vital things have been kept from them. And I want to change it."

Hector nodded slowly. "I still don't like you risking yourself so personally."

"Because... you love me," Rowena whispered.

Her heart started beating faster as she watched Hector. His gaze was steady on her as he nodded. And just like it had when he first said it, her heart soared.

"I love you, too," she blurted, afraid they'd be interrupted again.

Hector's eyes widened. "Wh-what?"

"I love you."

"But you said, to Lady Devonna—"

"I said that I married you for your connections," Rowena said. She reached for him, pulling him to sit with her on the couch. "Not that my feelings haven't grown and changed. I love you, Hector."

Hector grinned. He cupped her face in his hands and leaned in close. "Can I kiss you?"

"You don't have to ask," Rowena answered, tilting her face to his. "I always want you to kiss me."

So he did. Their arms wrapped around one another and the certainty of their situation grew stronger in Rowena's heart. They were meant to be together. And they would do good things for the kingdom.

CHAPTER

TWELVE

The next morning, Rowena and Hector shared a quick breakfast together before they had to separate for their duties. Hector carried the warmth of learning Rowena's true feelings for him throughout the difficulties he faced. The first was having to navigate the specifics of holding yet another official announcement, where he could reply to the concerns of the people.

Rowena would be working on inviting individuals to speak with her directly about the situation. It still made Hector nervous to think about her speaking face-to-face with people who may wish to do her harm. His protective instincts told him not to allow it.

But she was right. He needed to support her. He might not have learned a great deal about humans, but her explanation about strong convictions was something he heard fairly often. Humans were a balancing force for a reason.

He had to trust that the Earth was sharing what Rowena needed to do for her.

As he was in his study—it was even more cramped than Rowena's, but it was easier to write his speech in here rather than moving everything around to better accommodations—there was a knock on the door. A young, timid servant stepped in.

"Duke Volka to see you, your Royal Highness," the servant said. "He has Lord Corella with him."

Hector resisted the urge to tell the servant to send them away. Instead, he set his pen aside and nodded. "Show them in."

Part of supporting Rowena had to be standing in unity with her when she wasn't even here. No doubt Volka and Corella were plotting something. The two came in. Volka gave Hector a strained smile while Corella simply glared at him.

"Your Highness," Volka said with a stiff bow. "I've heard that the queen is inviting protestors to the palace and that you will be making an address to the people."

"You heard right."

Volka made a strangled noise. "You must see how foolhardy that is when there is already dissatisfaction. You are both presenting yourselves as targets."

"Not to mention, by you addressing this issue after already stating your piece, it will look even more like you are forcing Eldavon's morals onto Odentia," Corella added.

"No. It won't," Hector answered, rolling his eyes. He knew that it wasn't the best way to get through to them, but he was tired of this same argument. "The whole process must seem very strange and dangerous. I've explained, but it's clear that there is still a lack of understanding."

Volka shook his head, snorting. "You don't understand. The people are used to a strong hand ruling them. Take that hand away and they will strike back."

"And just why does strength have to be violent?" Hector demanded.

"They are like sheep," Corella argued. "You can't expect them to understand—"

"They're not sheep, they're people. I absolutely believe that every person is capable of understanding the truth of this matter, Lord Corella. Even you, despite all your attempts to keep yourself in ignorance," he added. Then he turned to Volka. "Is that a strong enough hand? Or do you only mean we should be causing physical harm to the most disenfranchised people in this kingdom?"

Volka leaned back in his chair, lacing his fingers over his stomach. "You aren't what I thought you would be."

"And what did you expect?" Hector asked, arching a brow at him.

Volka smiled. "Someone who only cared about his kingdom's ideals. But you actually care about our people too, don't you? You empathize with them."

"Of course I do. And so should you," Hector added. "What I don't quite understand is why you want to see them beaten down so badly. Do you miss the old king that much?"

"That is not what I mean." Volka's expression twisted. "I would never say that. What I mean is that you are taking people who have no sort of training in being leaders of society and giving them free rein. They won't know how to control themselves."

Corella nodded.

Hector studied Volka. "I see that it's you who doesn't understand what the Silver Springs are about. They may be witches, dragons, or humans. But going through the Springs doesn't mean they will run around doing whatever they want."

"And what's to stop them? You are from an influential family, so you were trained to be a dragon," Volka said.

"I was trained to understand what being a dragon means. The same training any of these dragons will get," Hector answered.

"It will be best if we could send our nobility, our leaders, through first," Volka insisted. "So that they can be there to guide the others."

So that's what it was about. Hector gazed back at Volka, the pieces clicking into place. It was all about control with Volka. Maybe he didn't wish for the old king back, but this whole thing was most certainly about control. He was offended that he wasn't in the first group chosen to go through the springs. Maybe he was afraid that he'd never get the chance.

"You're happy the protests are happening," Hector said, not losing eye contact. "Because it gives you more time to convince Rowena that you ought to go before anyone else. I just wonder... is it just you or do you think that this should be limited to your nobility?"

Volka's nostrils flared.

"You're afraid that if the people get any sort of power, they will return the same force you've used on them back on you," Hector continued.

"I have spent my life fighting for this kingdom," Volka snapped. "You know *nothing*."

Maybe he didn't know as much as he ought to. But he was working on that, and besides, he had knowledge in other areas.

"I know that I speak with the queen's authority when I say that we will not tolerate you attempting to undermine her decisions," Hector said, struggling to keep his voice cool. When he thought of protecting Rowena, he envisioned it as facing down enemies who meant her harm, not her own advisors. "I may not have been born to be a prince, but I am the queen's husband now."

Corella opened his mouth but stopped when Hector lifted his hand.

"Rowena knows what she wants for the people. It was free of interference by me. And if the culture you cling to is dependent on the hardship of others, Lord Corella, then perhaps it is a culture that should be done away with."

"How dare—"

Hector stood. Instantly, Corella shut his mouth.

"Odentia has so many beautiful, wonderful, and worthwhile traditions," Hector said, staring the two men down. "This kingdom has a long, proud heritage that should be celebrated. That doesn't mean there can't be positive changes made. The Queen wants a better, more prosperous future for this kingdom. And I will serve her with all my might and strength. "My loyalty is to her and the crown first and forever."

Corella opened and closed his mouth as though he wasn't sure what to say.

Volka, on the other hand, had gone stony-faced. His expression was difficult to read. "If this is true, then you must know that you need to proceed with caution. Nobody wants to see this rebellion turn into a civil war."

"Hence why we are combatting it by focusing on the root cause: misunderstanding," Hector answered. "And I'll start right now.

Bringing those people out there up to your level doesn't bring you down. You have valuable insights and experience in this kingdom. And so do they. Your problem is that you see all of this as there has to be a hierarchy of importance."

Volka frowned at him. "You have a lot of pretty words without understanding what our social system actually is."

Hector smiled. Oh, he could talk until he was blue in the face and they would never believe him. But he understood something better now, too. The reason why Rowena always commanded every room she was in.

"Let's go talk with the queen, then," he said, gesturing toward the door. "She is meeting with people to hear their worries. Perhaps, Duke Volka, it's time that you start being honest with your fears. You may find the answers more satisfactory."

"We're not interested," Corella started.

Volka shook his head as he stood. "Enough, Nathaniel. The Prince Consort is right. There has been far too much sneaking and secrecy in this palace. It's time we start trying to build trust."

Hector nodded toward him. "Let's go see Rowena, then. I'm sure she'll be much better with her words than I am."

CHAPTER
THIRTEEN

Rowena admired the way the sunlight glinted off Hector's styled hair as he stood on the balcony overlooking the plaza below. He wore the black and silver of Odentia today, but he seemed more at ease than usual.

Probably because one of his cousins, Aldon, had flown in as a dragon the previous night to drop off news of the rebels Eldavon had captured in their kingdom. Aldon had also brought with him the clothes Hector had sent weeks ago to have the spells needed to survive the shift to his dragon form. The dragon hadn't stuck around, as he was needed back in Eldavon, but Hector must be more comfortable knowing he could take his defensive form without destroying his clothes.

"The change is swift, but it's not painful," Hector was saying to the crowd. "Those who become dragons don't shift immediately. It takes some time for the dragon to mature and the shifting to start. It's always a voluntary process."

A red blob flew through the air. The tomato didn't reach the balcony, but it heralded the start of several groups hurling rotten vegetables toward them. Rowena stepped up next to Hector. The vegetables continued to fly, though none of them were anywhere close to hitting the two. People squealed and dodged the vegetables as they fell.

"Hugo, find them and bring them into the palace," Rowena murmured.

She took Hector's hand in her left, then raised her right toward the crowd. "Please remain calm. The Prince Consort has much more to explain."

Guards slipped between the people; several who were throwing vegetables yelped and tried to run, but they had anticipated this. Soon, everyone causing a disturbance had been rounded up. They were marched through the doors below the balcony.

"They will be released soon," Rowena said, her voice carrying over the crowd. "Don't be concerned for their safety. I merely wish to talk to them."

The people murmured to each other. Hector finished his speech and then Rowena spoke, once more explaining her convictions to improve Odentia's economy and societal well-being. Once she was done, they headed inside. The handful of people who'd been throwing vegetables waited in her parlor and had been served tea and sandwiches.

As she and Hector entered, one of them jumped to his feet. "It's my fault, I'm the one that convinced them—if anyone's gonna be punished, it's me!"

"What's your name?" Rowena asked.

"Chuck," the man replied nervously.

Rowena smiled at him. "Nobody is being punished today, Chuck. I want to know why you decided to throw vegetables at my husband."

Chuck shifted from foot to foot. He threw back his shoulders and pointed at Hector. "That dragon is blinding you. Eldavon is promising all this stuff, but they'll prevent anybody in Odentia from being dragons or witches. They'll stop it, mark my words."

"That's not how it works," Hector answered. "We don't decide what our fate is."

Chuck narrowed his eyes. "So you say. But if anyone was meant to be a dragon, it should be the queen! They stole it from her."

Hector shook his head. "No, that's not what it means. Rowena is human, connected to Earth magic."

"Liar!" one of the women screeched. She grabbed a sandwich off a tray and hurled it at Hector. "You're going to destroy Odentia! You'll never even let us defend ourselves."

Hector batted away the squishy projectiles. "If you'll just listen to me—"

"We're done listening!" Chuck howled. "It's you that turned the queen against Prince Finnegan! He always fought for us low people and you have him locked away!"

Rowena turned toward Hugo. "Go fetch the Gorgon mirror from my chambers."

Hugo stared at her. "Your Majesty, I can't—"

"Go," Rowena ordered.

He glanced at the people, then bowed briefly and left, walking quickly.

"My uncle is not locked away," Rowena said. "He was cursed by a wicked wizard, Silas. He now lives at the Silver Springs in Eldavon. Those selected by the lottery will see him themselves. In the meantime, if you want proof of his life, I have the means of talking with him."

"More lies!" The woman grabbed the delicate teapot and hurled it at Hector's head.

He jumped aside but the others followed suit, grabbing anything they could get their hands on to throw at Hector. He grabbed a silver platter and held it as a shield. When Chuck grabbed a fire poker, Rowena had had enough. She didn't know if they were genuine about their concern for her or Finnegan, but she did know something—they were afraid.

Just like she had been terrified of Eldavon and its dragons.

Because she had been taught to fear them because her father had done his best to make sure that everyone would think his plans for war were justified.

She held out her hands, breathing deeply. The strength and connection she felt to the earth flared through her. It calmed the thoughts in her mind and flowed throw her body. She knew instantly exactly what she needed to do, and she strode forward. Chuck hesitated. The door opened and Hugo came back in. Seeing the man with the fire poker lifted toward the queen, he yelled and started to draw his sword.

Rowena didn't stop.

She stepped up to Chuck and took hold of the poker, lowering it. Then she smiled at him and drew him into a hug.

Chuck let out a surprised huff.

"I know you're afraid," Rowena said. She stepped away from him and turned to the woman, embracing her. "It sounds impossible to be human and have anything to stand against a dragon."

She moved down the line, embracing each in turn. When she was done, she stood before them and held her hands outstretched. "Do you feel that? The power in this room? The feeling of calm and peace?"

Hugo released the hilt of his sword, staring at Rowena in wonderment. Hector, on the other hand, beamed at her.

Rowena took a moment to smile back at him. Chuck and the others stared at her in wonder. Once, she would have thought it was just because of her actions. But she knew better now. It might be difficult to trust her instincts when for so much of her life she was denied them, but things were changing... for the better.

"This is what it means to be human," she said, lowering her arms. "This is what it means to have Earth magic. We are the ones with our feet firmly on the ground. We are the ones that can see the most clearly.

"Oh, it's not as flashy as being a dragon or as noticeable as being a witch," Rowena continued with a soft chuckle, "but that's the point. We don't need to be flashy or noticeable to be just as important. Humans have always been grounded. We are a balancing power in the world. The Silver Springs doesn't change who we are; it reveals a deeper understanding of who we are."

Chuck started to kneel but Rowena caught his hand and shook her head.

"If there's one thing I've learned from this strange new power, it's that our natural state is equality." She smiled at him. "Otherwise, why would we have to fight so hard to keep these systems of hierarchy in place?"

Chuck bowed his head. "I... I understand. I didn't before but I do now."

"You're lucky."

Rowena thought of her discussion with Duke Volka and Lord Corella. Volka had seemed to try to understand and eventually agreed that he could perhaps try harder. Corella, on the other hand, simply refused. He had made up his mind to willfully misunderstand what the process was and therefore would never change his mind.

"Odentia has been in pain for a long, long time," Rowena said. She smiled over her shoulder and reached for Hector's hands. "And thanks to Eldavon, we will finally start healing. All we need now is trust."

CHAPTER

FOURTEEN

I t wasn't easy, but things did end up settling down. The rebel attacks dwindled until they almost disappeared entirely. Rowena was in the process of having the prison system reformed as well, although they all knew that would be far more difficult than the problems they had faced so far.

Hector had completely forgotten about the fact that Rowena wanted to host a ball to present him as Prince Consort until they were a week out from the ball itself. Then, he had a frantic dash to learn everything he needed to learn for the event, as well as help with the final preparations.

It was hectic, but he loved it. Mostly because it gave him more of an excuse to spend time with Rowena.

The ball was held at the palace. As Hector strode in, escorting Rowena, the sight took his breath away. The walls had been decorated in black and silver. Rather than the moons that were traditional, however, the silver on these banners were embroidered dragons, cradling a golden sun protectively at its heart. A crescent moon had been painted on the floor.

Rowena smiled at him, leading the way down one of the massive staircases. He wore an elaborate outfit; a black tunic with billowing sleeves, over which was a fitted silver vest, with moons for buttons. A bright red dragon, the same color as his own, was embroidered to be wrapped around him. His boots, too, were emblazed with silver dragons.

"Thank you all for being here," Rowena called when they reached a landing just before the final few steps to the ballroom. "I present to you my husband, the Prince Consort Hector."

There was a polite smattering of applause. Hector bowed toward the crowd, then bowed to Rowena and knelt to one knee.

"I am humbled to be here, chosen to serve you," he said, his voice carrying through the room. "From this day and forever more, I vow to serve well. I will follow you and your commands until I draw my final breath. This solemn oath I swear upon sun and stars. You are my queen and my light."

Rowena took his hand and lifted him back to his feet. Another round of applause sounded, louder this time. Hector leaned forward, pressing a gentle kiss to his wife's lips.

The cheers erupted. Rowena laughed into his kiss.

As they stepped into the crowd and people began to flatter them, Hector only had eyes for her. She was stunning in a deep green gown that fit against her frame perfectly. Her long black curls hung loose, making her look like something out of a fairy tale. And she had chosen him. Hector could hardly believe it.

They had accomplished so much. And he looked forward to all the days ahead of them where they would accomplish more.

Only last week, they had held the second lottery for the next hundred citizens of Odentia to travel to the Silver Springs. The first trials were such a success that only three of the newly selected people refused this time.

Everyone who had been selected for the second Silver Springs caravan was in attendance, as were those who had gone through the first time. From that first batch came four dragons and three witches. They were only back to Odentia briefly before they would return to Eldavon to start their training.

It was going well. Hector stopped next to one of the first who went through the Springs. Visually, she looked much the same as she had when she left. Her cheeks were fuller, her hair thicker and shinier, and she seemed overall more vibrant, but that was in large part due to the fact that she was no longer malnourished.

"How are you doing?" Hector asked her.

She beamed at him as she curtsied. "Excellently, Your Highness. I've learned so much on this journey."

"I'm glad to hear it. Is there anything in particular you learned?"

"Too much to express in words. I understand myself and this world so much better. I can look through this crowd and I just know who is in pain, who needs help. Who I can help," she answered, her gaze skimming over the patrons. "Its..."

She struggled with what to say.

Hector chuckled. "Overwhelming and exhilarating?"

"Those are good words."

A waltz started to play and Hector turned to Rowena. She had the same idea and they stepped out onto the dance floor, leading the first dance of the night. As the music started, Hector put his arms around her and they spun off, twirling across the floor.

"You are magnificent," Rowena breathed.

Hector laughed. "I was about to say the exact same thing to you."

"Mmmm, good thing I claimed it first, then," Rowena teased. "You'll have to figure out some other way to compliment me."

"Wonderful? Awe-inspiring? The most beautiful woman to ever set foot on land?" Hector asked.

Rowena blushed. "Oh, I wouldn't go that far."

Hector laughed again. They danced together for two songs before they reluctantly parted to socialize with their guests again. Duke Volka approached Hector, tapping his cane against the floor as he walked.

"Your Royal Highness," he greeted with a nod of his head. He viewed the dance with a small smile on his face, resting against his cane. "It seems you have grown admirably well into this role."

"Thank you, Your Grace," Hector answered.

Volka nodded once and turned toward him. "Thank *you*. For being more interested in making sure I understood what you were saying over being right. I can be a pigheaded fool, I acknowledge this, but I'm not so proud that I can't say I was wrong. In this scenario, at least."

Hector nodded his acknowledgment.

THE BALL LASTED LATE into the night. After the guests had all left, Rowena and Hector returned to their room. Though they still had their separate chambers for when they needed space, Hector had moved his few personal belongings into Rowena's chambers. They liked to be close together.

"That went wonderfully," Hector said once they were alone.

Rowena nodded as she turned her back to him. "Help me out of all these buttons, will you?"

Hector grinned, unbuttoning the tiny things. Rowena swept her hair out of the way and sighed as the tight gown loosened.

"I'm not looking forward to getting a whole new wardrobe," she sighed.

"A new wardrobe?" Hector frowned. She had many beautiful dresses already. "Why do you need a new wardrobe?"

He helped her take off the heavy outer layer. Rowena turned to him, her shift loose around her. She smiled up at him as she took his hand and pressed it to her stomach, just below her stays.

"Because soon they will all be too small for me to wear."

She guided his hand over the subtle swell of her stomach. Hector gasped, his eyes widening.

"You're pregnant?"

Rowena laughed and wrapped her arms around him. "Yes. I figured it out this morning. I've been dying all day to tell you."

Hector beamed at her. He kissed her lightly, holding her tight. The future looked bright indeed, united by peace at last.

"I love you," he murmured into her lips.

"I love you, too."

THE END

If you enjoyed this book, please consider leaving a review on
Goodreads, Bookbub or your favorite retailer.
Reviews help me reach new readers.

**Join my newsletter for writing updates, sneak peaks, review
copies, sales, and giveaways!
www.mhlebeault.com**